THE BIG SWEEP

Based on the TV series *Nickelodeon Rocket Power*® created by Klasky Csupo, Inc. as seen on Nickelodeon®

SIMON SPOTLIGHT
An imprint of Simon & Schuster Children's Publishing Division
1230 Avenue of the Americas, New York, New York 10020

First Edition   10 9 8 7 6 5 4 3 2 1

Library of Congress Cataloging-in-Publication Data
Dubowski, Cathy East
The big sweep / by Cathy East Dubowski and Mark Dubowski.— 1st ed.
p. cm. — (Rocket Power ready-to-read. Level 2 ; #3)
"Based on the TV series Nickelodeon Rocket PowerTM created by Klasky Csupo, Inc. as seen on Nickelodeon."
Summary: Otto competes in a street hockey game with Lars, who has a new and expensive hockey stick.
ISBN 0-689-85831-0 (pbk. : alk. paper)
[1. Hockey—Fiction.] I. Dubowski, Mark. II. Nickelodeon rocket power (Television program) III. Title. IV. Series.
PZ7.D85445Bi 2003
[E]—dc21
2003005714

NICKELODEON
ROCKET POWER ™

THE BIG SWEEP

by
Kathy East Dubowski
and Mark Dubowski

illustrated by
Artful Doodlers Ltd.

Simon Spotlight/Nickelodeon
New York   London   Toronto   Sydney   Singapore

"Awesome," Otto said as he stared
at the new street hockey sticks.
"Iceman sticks!"

"Iceman is the greatest hockey player
of all time," Otto said.
"No wonder his sticks
cost so much,"
said Twister.

Just then someone reached in
and took a stick from the display!

It was Lars!
Otto groaned. "Lars is getting the Iceman stick! Now we will never beat him in a game!"

"Hey, why the long face, brudda?"
Tito asked Otto.
"The new Iceman hockey stick
just came out,"
Otto said.
"And I need it—bad."
"Well, then, you need a job,"
Tito said.

Otto swept for hours.
"Shoobies sure are messy," he said.

Finally the Shore Shack closed.
Otto rushed over to Madtown
to meet his friends.

But when Otto got to Madtown
it was too late.
"We can still have fun,"
Reggie said.

Reggie and Otto played Ping-Pong
with flyswatters.
Reggie called it ping-swat.

Sam and Twister played basketball
with a paper bag.
Sam called it trashketball.

Then Lars showed up.
"Hey, Otto, want to get iced?"
he asked, showing off
his new Iceman stick.

"Who needs that?" Otto said.
"I could beat you
with a **broom**stick!"
"Prove it!" Lars said.

The next day Otto and Lars
faced off in the parking lot.

Lars threw down a puck.
Otto picked up his broom.
"Ready?" Lars asked.
"Go!" Otto yelled.

The game was on!

Lars scored the first point.

Then Otto got a point.

Lars got the next point.

Then Otto
scored again!

The game was tied.
"Five seconds left!" Sam yelled.
Otto skated hard.
Lars tried to get in his way.

Then Otto fired a sweep shot—
right past Lars!
"Goal!" Twister yelled.
"Otto wins!" Reggie yelled.

The next day everyone
was at the Shore Shack.
"I could have won,"
Lars told Otto. "Except for
my skates. I need new ones."

Otto smiled.

"I can help you, Lars," he said.

Otto looked at Tito.
"Lars needs a job, so he can buy
new skates," he said.
"If it's okay with you,
he can have mine!"

Later Twister asked Otto,
"Why did you give your job to Lars?"
"I want to hold on to
    my old hockey stick," Otto said.
"And I want Lars to hold on to
    my old broomstick."

Twister scratched his head.
Otto smiled. "Lars will get it."

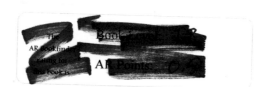